Y

Jefferson Twp Public Library
1031 Weldon Road
Oak Ridge, N.J. 07438
APR 2012
973-208-6244
www.jeffersonlibrary.net

1. Most items may be checked out ████████ and renewed for the same period. Additional restrictions may apply to high-demand items.

2. A fine is charged for each day material is not returned according to the above rule. No material will be issued to any person incurring such a fine until it has been paid.

3. All damage to material beyond reasonable wear and all losses shall be paid for.

4. Each borrower is responsible for all items checked out on his/her library card and for all fines accruing on the same.

STAR WARS®
KNIGHT ERRANT
AFLAME

VOLUME FOUR

SCRIPT
JOHN JACKSON MILLER

PENCILS
IVAN RODRIGUEZ

INKS
IVAN RODRIGUEZ
BELARDINO BRABO

COLORS
MICHAEL ATIYEH

LETTERING
MICHAEL HEISLER

COVER ART
JOE QUINONES

When she arrived on Chelloa to strike a blow against the Sith, Kerra Holt became trapped in a war between two Sith Lords. After foiling an attempt by the nihilistic Lord Odion to destroy the planet's surface, Kerra traveled to his interstellar war forge, hoping to prevent a second try.

But before Odion could goad Kerra into making a suicidal attack, his brother and enemy, Lord Daiman, sent a message. He had captured the informant responsible for bringing Odion to Chelloa—Gorlan Palladane, friend to the people of Chelloa, and, Kerra knew, secretly a former Jedi!

Puzzled by the news—and fearing a purge against Gorlan's people—Kerra fled from Odion's presence. But while her venture against Odion failed to deter him from returning to Chelloa, it has changed his plans. Odion will return to Chelloa not to destroy it, but to it . . .

This story takes place approximately 1,032 years BBY.

DARK HORSE COMICS

Spotlight

visit us at www.abdopublishing.com

Reinforced library bound edition published in 2012 by Spotlight,
a division of the ABDO Group, PO Box 398166, Minneapolis, MN 55439.
Spotlight produces high-quality reinforced library bound editions for schools and libraries.
Published by agreement with Dark Horse Comics, Inc., and Lucasfilm Ltd.

Printed in the United States of America, North Mankato, Minnesota.
102011
012012
This book contains at least 10% recycled materials.

Library of Congress Cataloging-in-Publication Data

Miller, John Jackson.
  Star wars : knight errant. volume 1 Aflame / script, John Jackson Miller ; pencils, Federico
Dallocchio. -- Reinforced library bound ed.
    p. cm.
  "Dark Horse."
  "LucasFilm."
  Summary: Eighteen-year-old Kerra Holt, a Jedi Knight on her first mission, is left deep in
Sith space without any support or resources and realizes how unprepared she is, but will not
abandon the Jedi's mission to help the colony.
  ISBN 978-1-59961-986-6 (volume 1) -- ISBN 978-1-59961-987-3 (volume 2)
  ISBN 978-1-59961-988-0 (volume 3) -- ISBN 978-1-59961-989-7 (volume 4)
  ISBN 978-1-59961-990-3 (volume 5)
  1. Graphic novels. [1. Graphic novels. 2. Science fiction.] I. Dallocchio, Federico, ill. II. Title.
III. Title: Knight errant. IV. Title: Aflame.
  PZ7.7.M535St 2012
  741.5'973--dc23
                    2011031240

All Spotlight books are reinforced library binding
and manufactured in the United States of America.

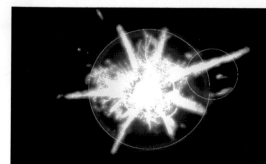

"I WAS BORED --

"-- AND SO I CREATED THE UNIVERSE.

"I HAVE NO DIRECT KNOWLEDGE OF THE TIME BEFORE TIME. BUT I INFER THAT WHEREVER I WAS, NOTHING COULD CHALLENGE ME.

"AND SO I CREATED A *NEW* EXISTENCE. ALL MATTER, ALL ENERGY ARE MANIFESTATIONS OF MY UNDYING SPIRIT.

"BUT WHILE I GAVE ALL BEINGS MOTION, NOT ALL BEINGS SERVE ME. FOR I ALSO CREATED AN OPPONENT -- IN *ODION.*

"HE CLAIMS HE IS MY OLDER BROTHER -- BUT I, OF COURSE, HAVE NO KIN OR KIND. HE IS SIMPLY WHAT I MUST OVERCOME TO *ADVANCE.*

"AND NOW I LEARN THAT *YOU* STAND WITH HIM, RATHER THAN WITH *LORD DAIMAN,* WHO GAVE YOU LIFE.

"YOU OFFEND CREATION -- *MY CREATION.* SO NOW, *GORLAN PALLADANE* --"

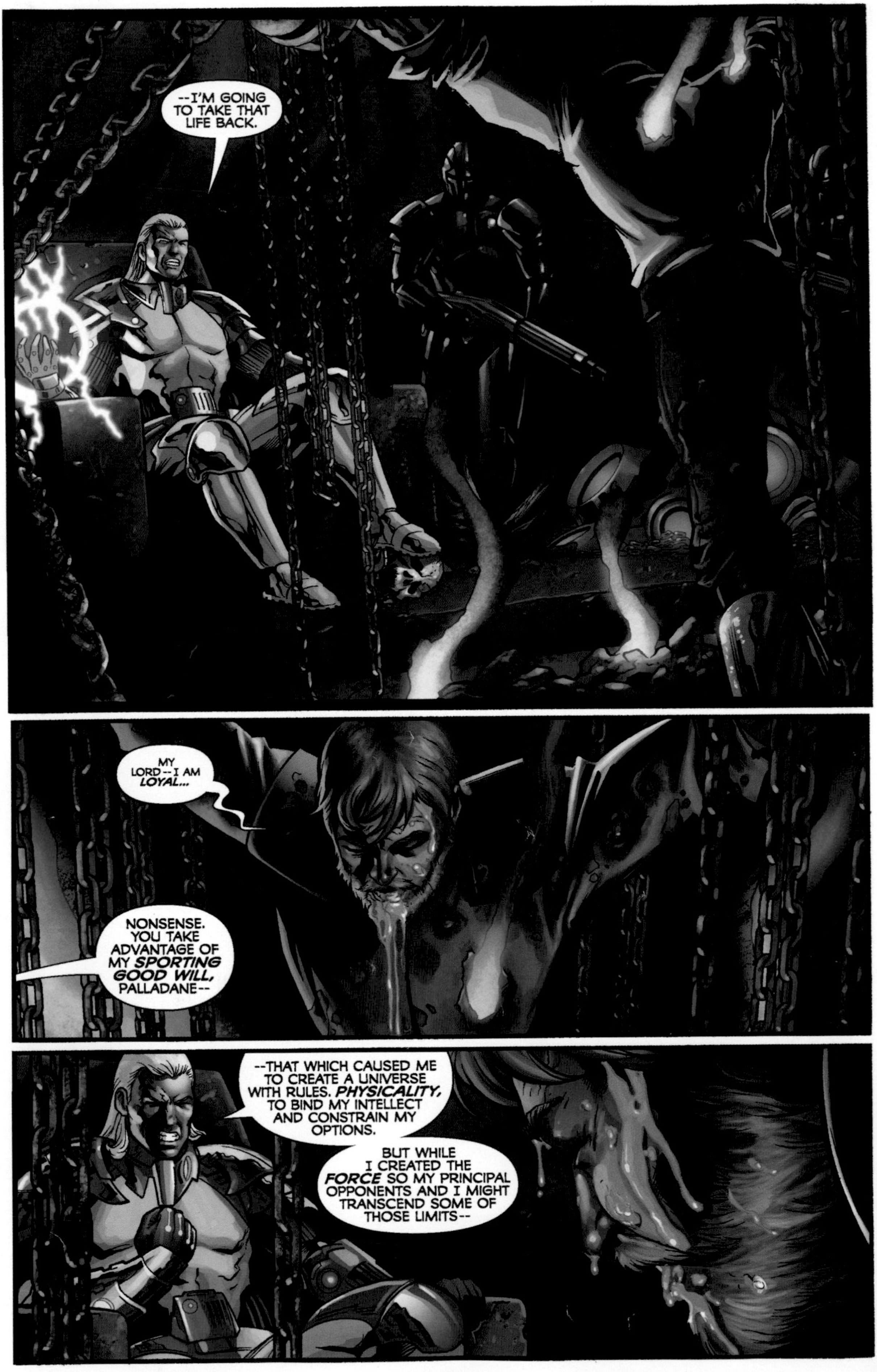
--I'M GOING TO TAKE THAT LIFE BACK.
MY LORD-- I AM *LOYAL...*
NONSENSE. YOU TAKE ADVANTAGE OF MY *SPORTING GOOD WILL,* PALLADANE--
--THAT WHICH CAUSED ME TO CREATE A UNIVERSE WITH RULES. *PHYSICALITY,* TO BIND MY INTELLECT AND CONSTRAIN MY OPTIONS.
BUT WHILE I CREATED THE *FORCE* SO MY PRINCIPAL OPPONENTS AND I MIGHT TRANSCEND SOME OF THOSE LIMITS--

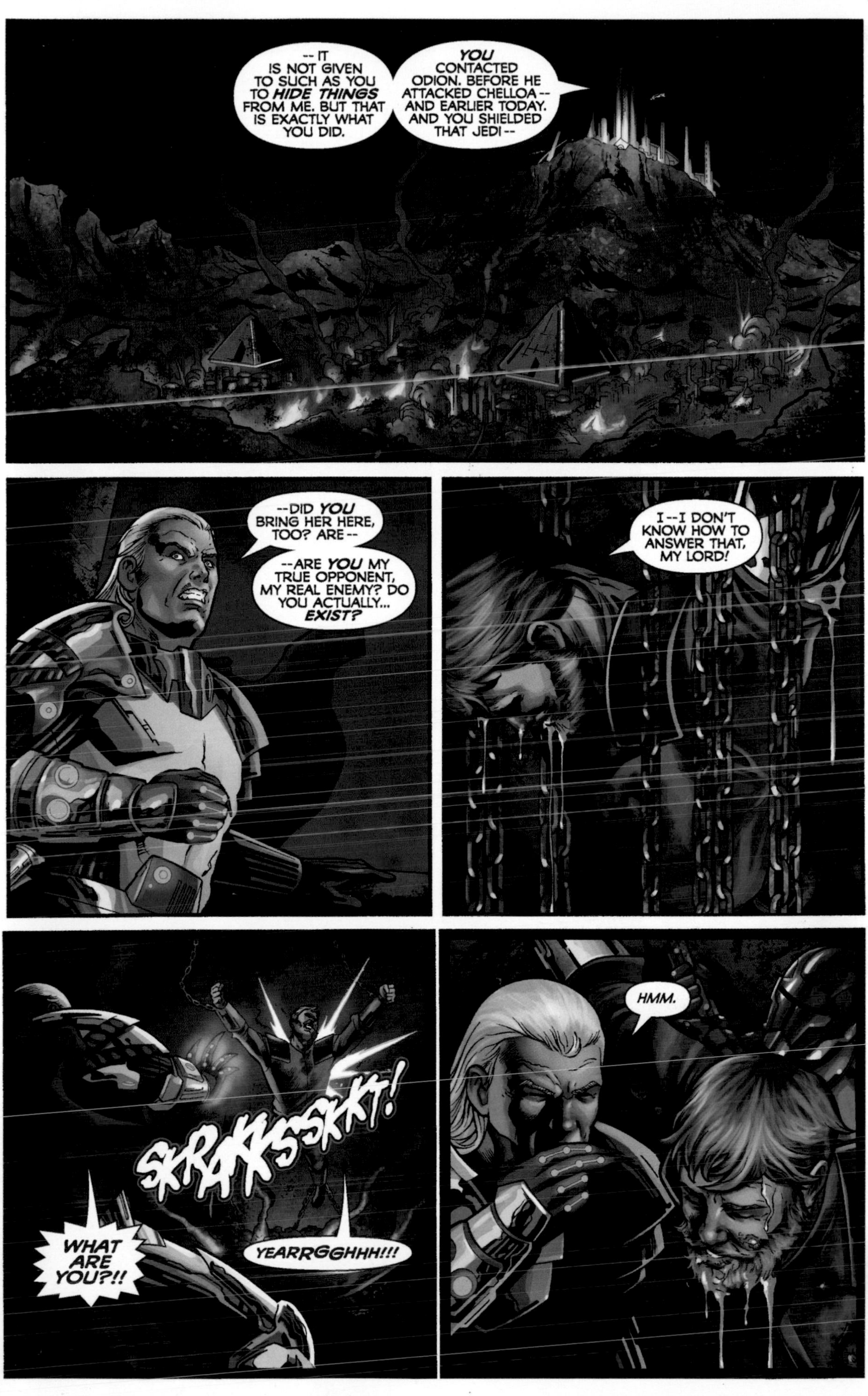
-- IT IS NOT GIVEN TO SUCH AS YOU TO HIDE THINGS FROM ME. BUT THAT IS EXACTLY WHAT YOU DID.
YOU CONTACTED ODION. BEFORE HE ATTACKED CHELLOA -- AND EARLIER TODAY. AND YOU SHIELDED THAT JEDI --
--DID YOU BRING HER HERE, TOO? ARE --
--ARE YOU MY TRUE OPPONENT, MY REAL ENEMY? DO YOU ACTUALLY... EXIST?
I -- I DON'T KNOW HOW TO ANSWER THAT, MY LORD!
SKRAKKSSKKT!
WHAT ARE YOU?!!
YEARRGGHHH!!!
HMM.

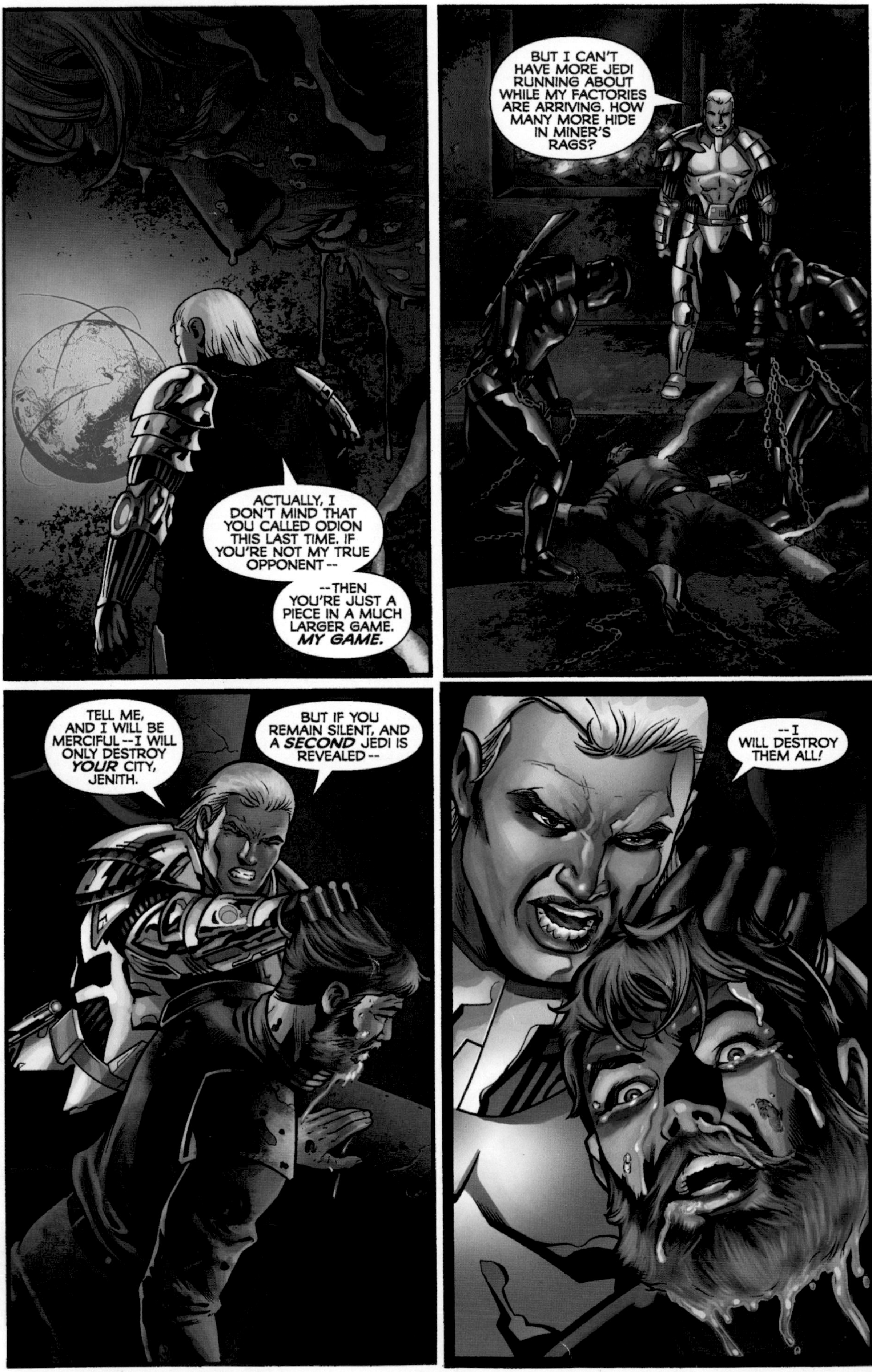
ACTUALLY, I DON'T MIND THAT YOU CALLED ODION THIS LAST TIME. IF YOU'RE NOT MY TRUE OPPONENT--
--THEN YOU'RE JUST A PIECE IN A MUCH LARGER GAME. MY GAME.
BUT I CAN'T HAVE MORE JEDI RUNNING ABOUT WHILE MY FACTORIES ARE ARRIVING. HOW MANY MORE HIDE IN MINER'S RAGS?
TELL ME, AND I WILL BE MERCIFUL--I WILL ONLY DESTROY YOUR CITY, JENITH.
BUT IF YOU REMAIN SILENT, AND A SECOND JEDI IS REVEALED--
--I WILL DESTROY THEM ALL!

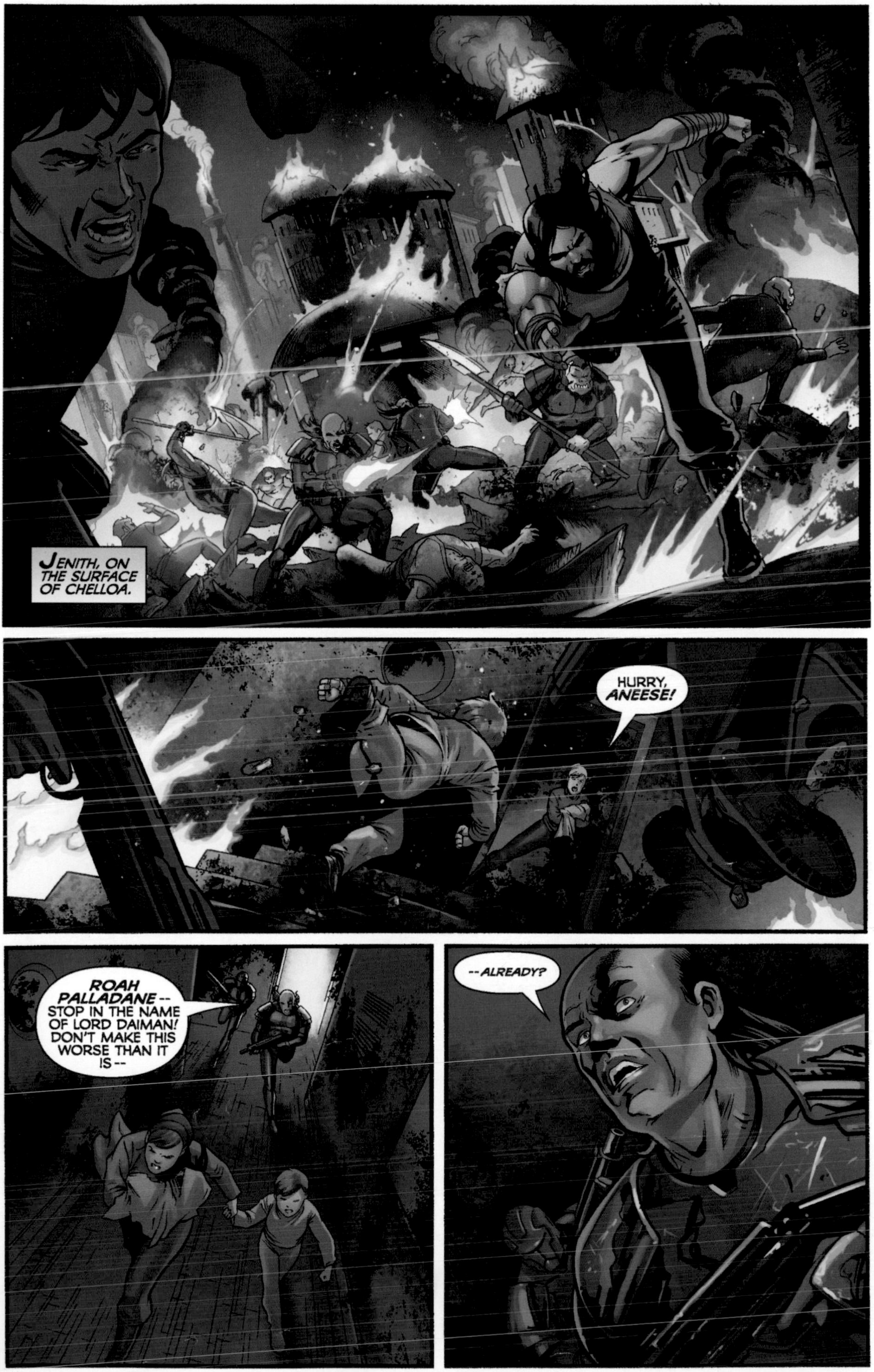
JENITH, ON THE SURFACE OF CHELLOA.
HURRY, ANEESE!
ROAH PALLADANE -- STOP IN THE NAME OF LORD DAIMAN! DON'T MAKE THIS WORSE THAN IT IS --
-- ALREADY?

GET OUT OF THEIR HOME.

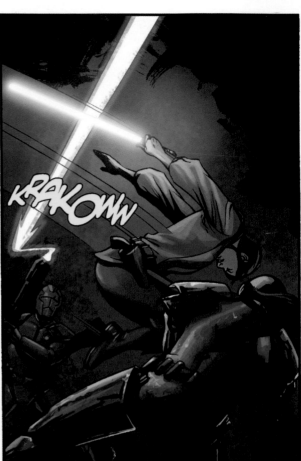

KRAKOWW

GAAAHH!

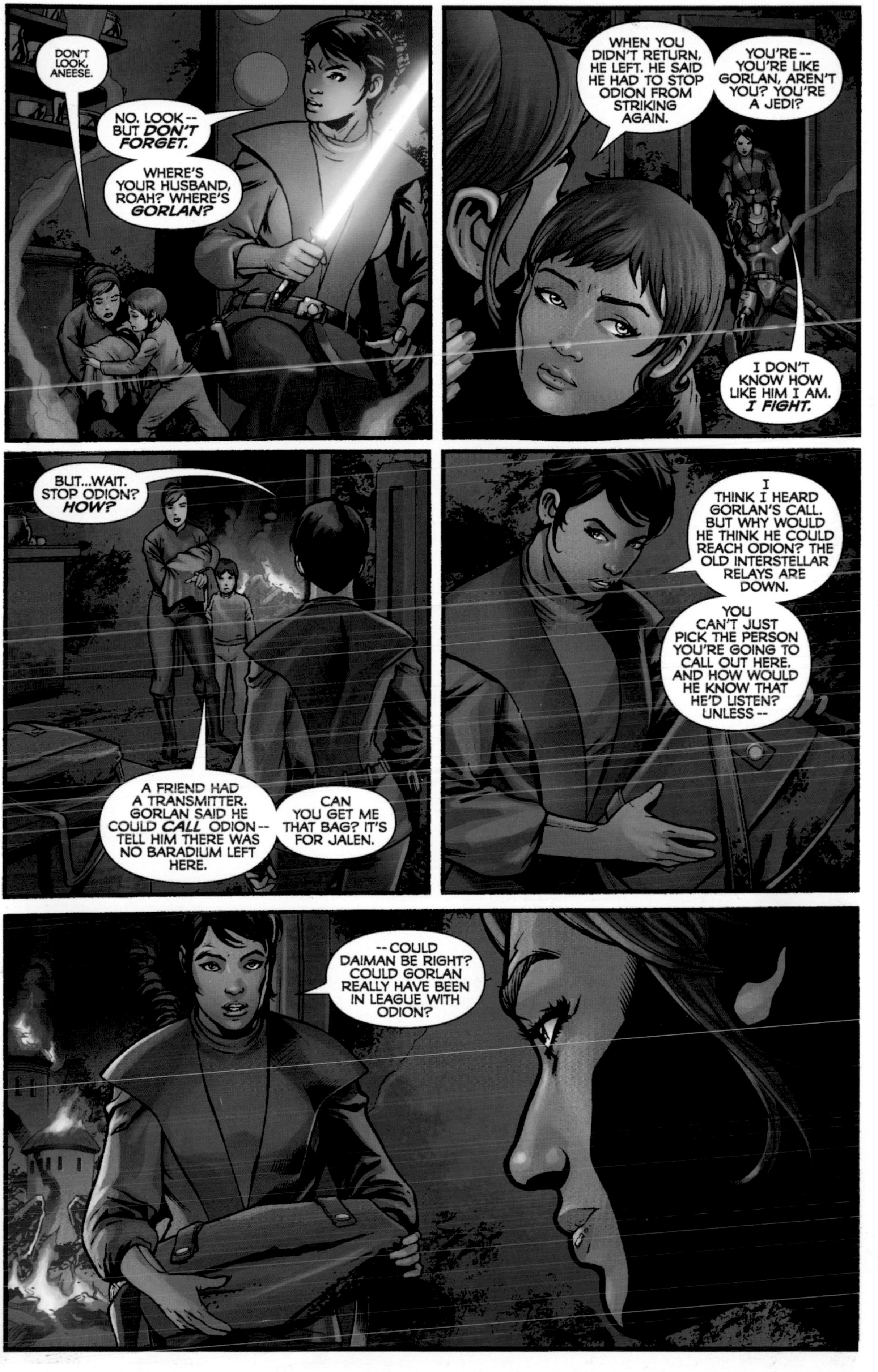
DON'T LOOK, ANEESE.
NO. LOOK -- BUT DON'T FORGET.
WHERE'S YOUR HUSBAND, ROAH? WHERE'S GORLAN?
WHEN YOU DIDN'T RETURN, HE LEFT. HE SAID HE HAD TO STOP ODION FROM STRIKING AGAIN.
YOU'RE -- YOU'RE LIKE GORLAN, AREN'T YOU? YOU'RE A JEDI?
I DON'T KNOW HOW LIKE HIM I AM. I FIGHT.
BUT...WAIT. STOP ODION? HOW?
A FRIEND HAD A TRANSMITTER. GORLAN SAID HE COULD CALL ODION -- TELL HIM THERE WAS NO BARADIUM LEFT HERE.
CAN YOU GET ME THAT BAG? IT'S FOR JALEN.
I THINK I HEARD GORLAN'S CALL. BUT WHY WOULD HE THINK HE COULD REACH ODION? THE OLD INTERSTELLAR RELAYS ARE DOWN.
YOU CAN'T JUST PICK THE PERSON YOU'RE GOING TO CALL OUT HERE. AND HOW WOULD HE KNOW THAT HE'D LISTEN? UNLESS --
-- COULD DAIMAN BE RIGHT? COULD GORLAN REALLY HAVE BEEN IN LEAGUE WITH ODION?

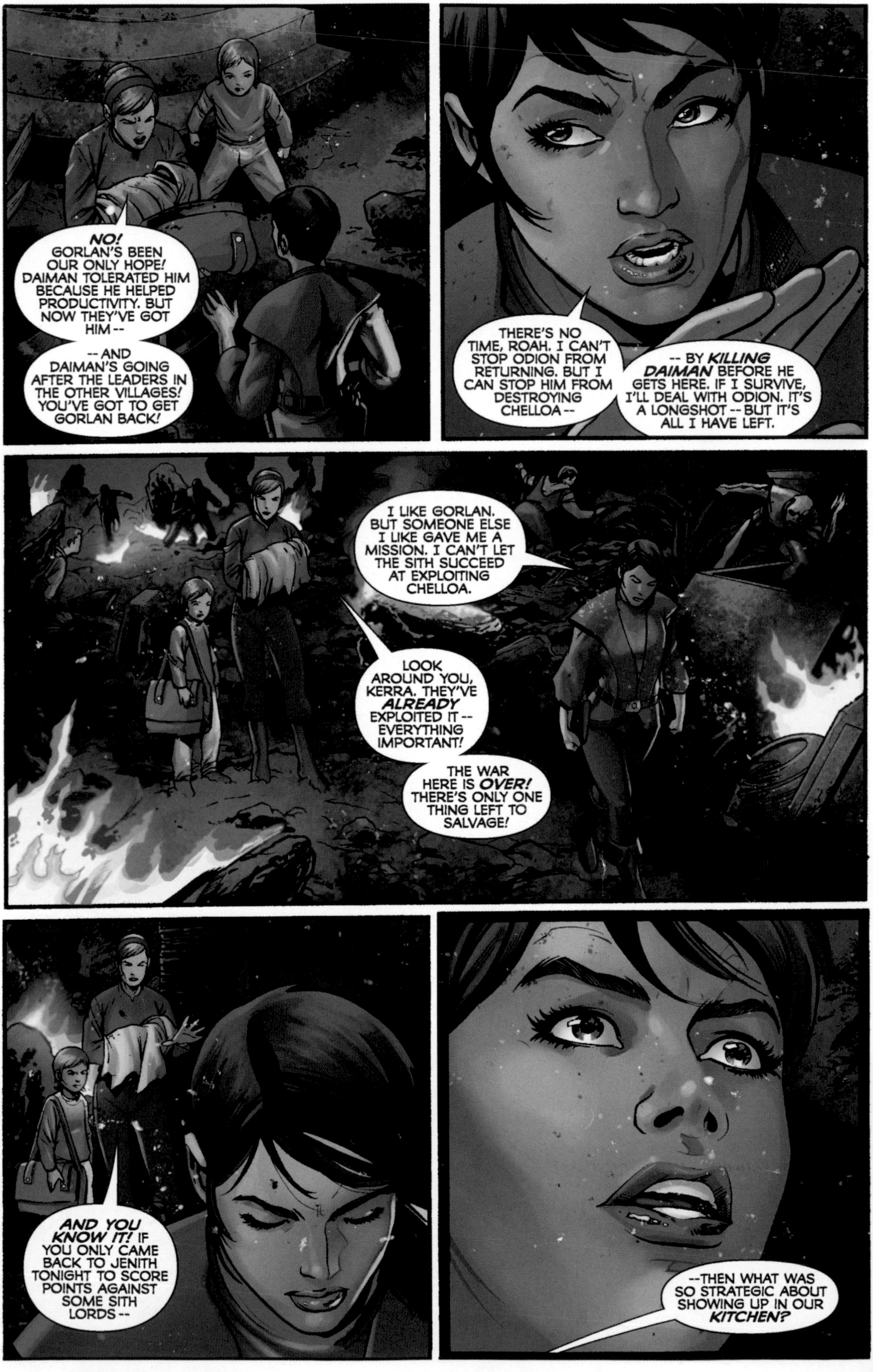
NO! GORLAN'S BEEN OUR ONLY HOPE! DAIMAN TOLERATED HIM BECAUSE HE HELPED PRODUCTIVITY. BUT NOW THEY'VE GOT HIM --
-- AND DAIMAN'S GOING AFTER THE LEADERS IN THE OTHER VILLAGES! YOU'VE GOT TO GET GORLAN BACK!
THERE'S NO TIME, ROAH. I CAN'T STOP ODION FROM RETURNING. BUT I CAN STOP HIM FROM DESTROYING CHELLOA --
-- BY KILLING DAIMAN BEFORE HE GETS HERE. IF I SURVIVE, I'LL DEAL WITH ODION. IT'S A LONGSHOT -- BUT IT'S ALL I HAVE LEFT.
I LIKE GORLAN. BUT SOMEONE ELSE I LIKE GAVE ME A MISSION. I CAN'T LET THE SITH SUCCEED AT EXPLOITING CHELLOA.
LOOK AROUND YOU, KERRA. THEY'VE ALREADY EXPLOITED IT -- EVERYTHING IMPORTANT!
THE WAR HERE IS OVER! THERE'S ONLY ONE THING LEFT TO SALVAGE!
AND YOU KNOW IT! IF YOU ONLY CAME BACK TO JENITH TONIGHT TO SCORE POINTS AGAINST SOME SITH LORDS --
--THEN WHAT WAS SO STRATEGIC ABOUT SHOWING UP IN OUR KITCHEN?

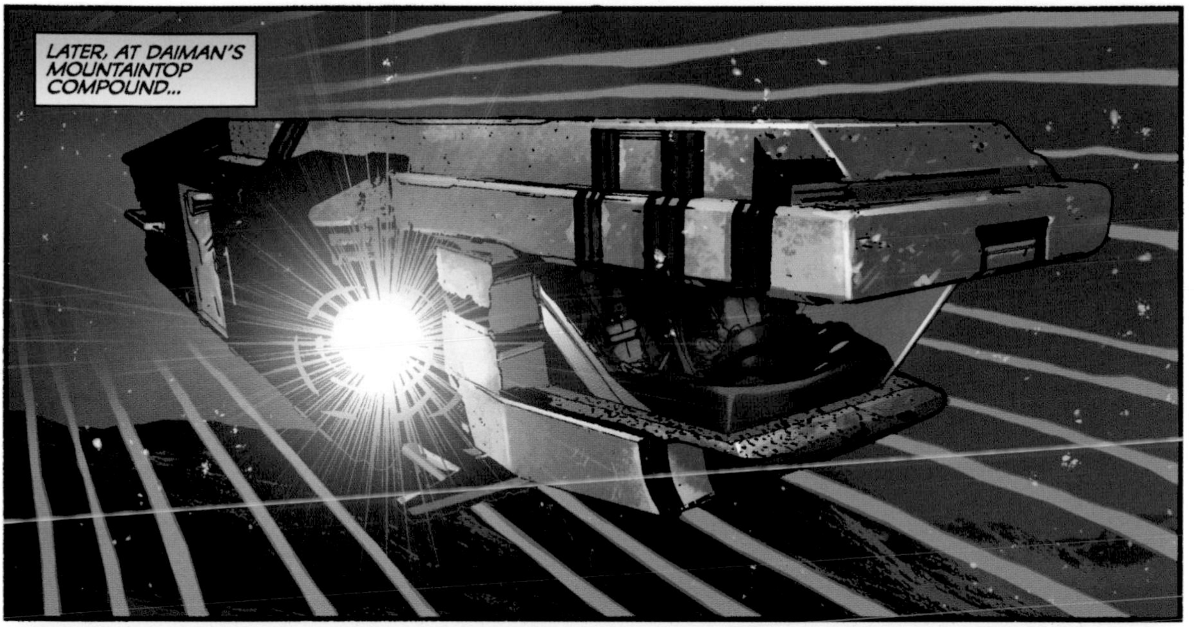
LATER, AT DAIMAN'S MOUNTAINTOP COMPOUND...

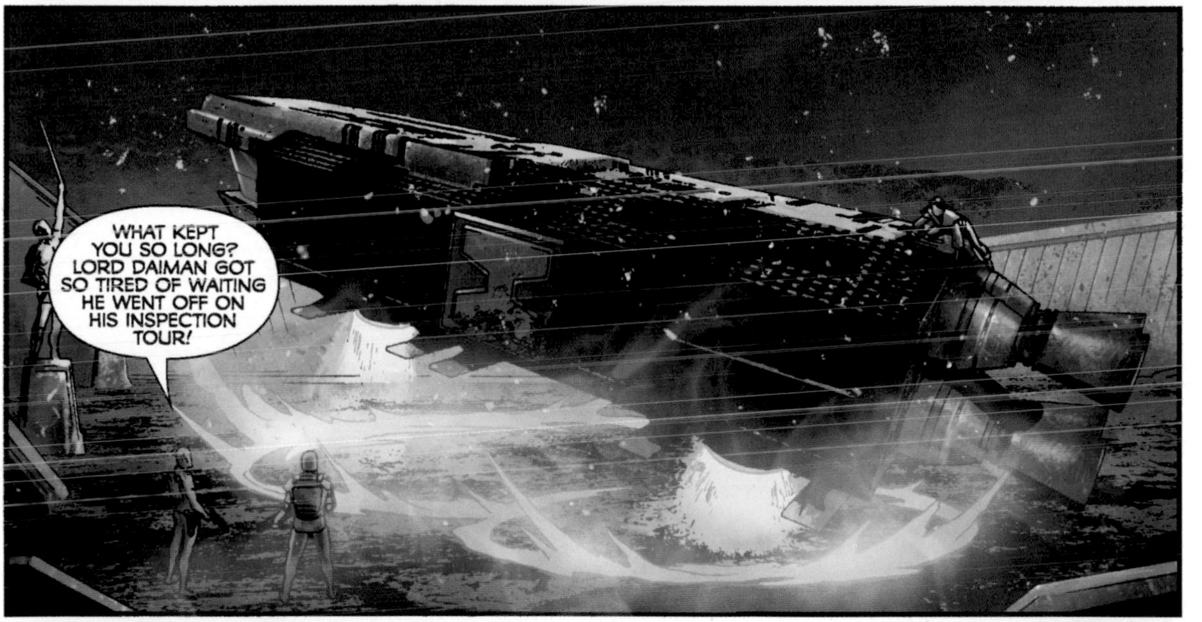
WHAT KEPT YOU SO LONG? LORD DAIMAN GOT SO TIRED OF WAITING HE WENT OFF ON HIS INSPECTION TOUR!

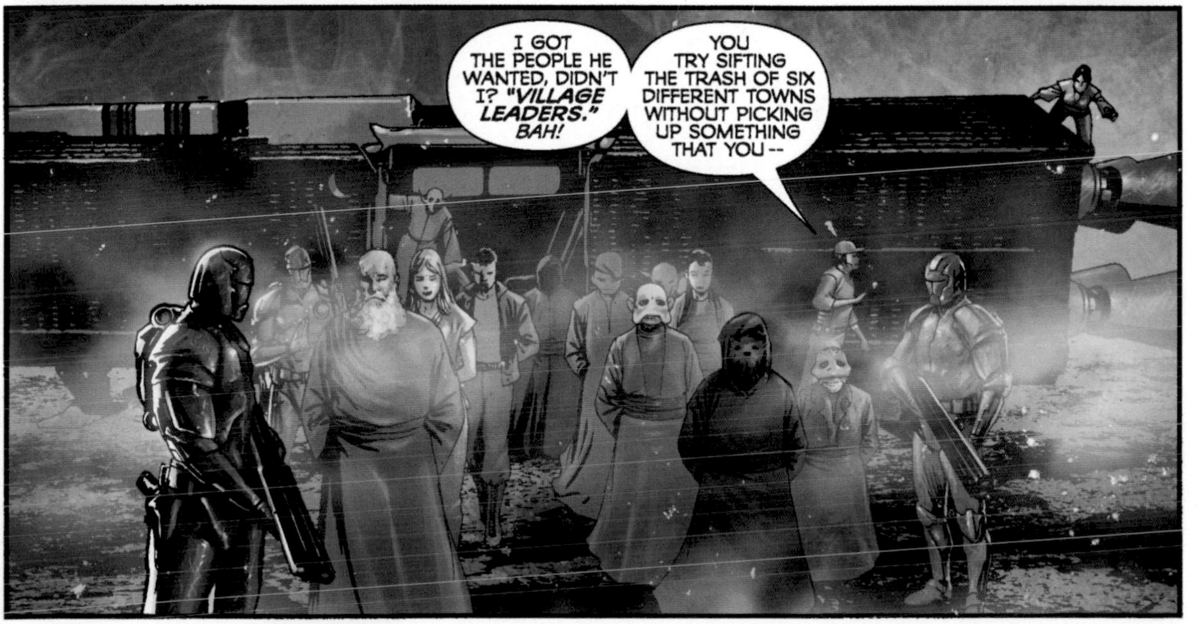
I GOT THE PEOPLE HE WANTED, DIDN'T I? "VILLAGE LEADERS." BAH!
YOU TRY SIFTING THE TRASH OF SIX DIFFERENT TOWNS WITHOUT PICKING UP SOMETHING THAT YOU --

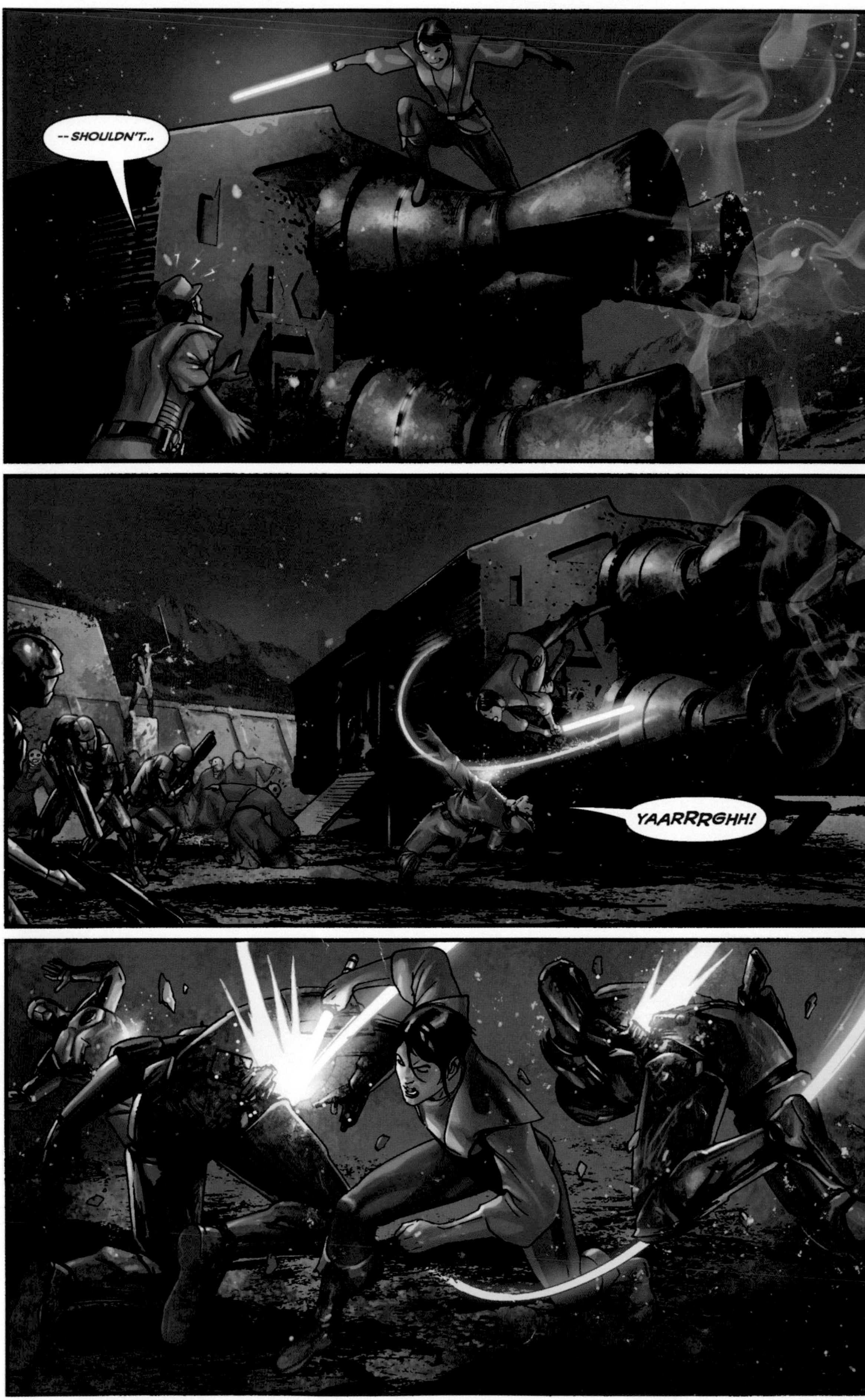
--SHOULDN'T...
YAARRRGHH!

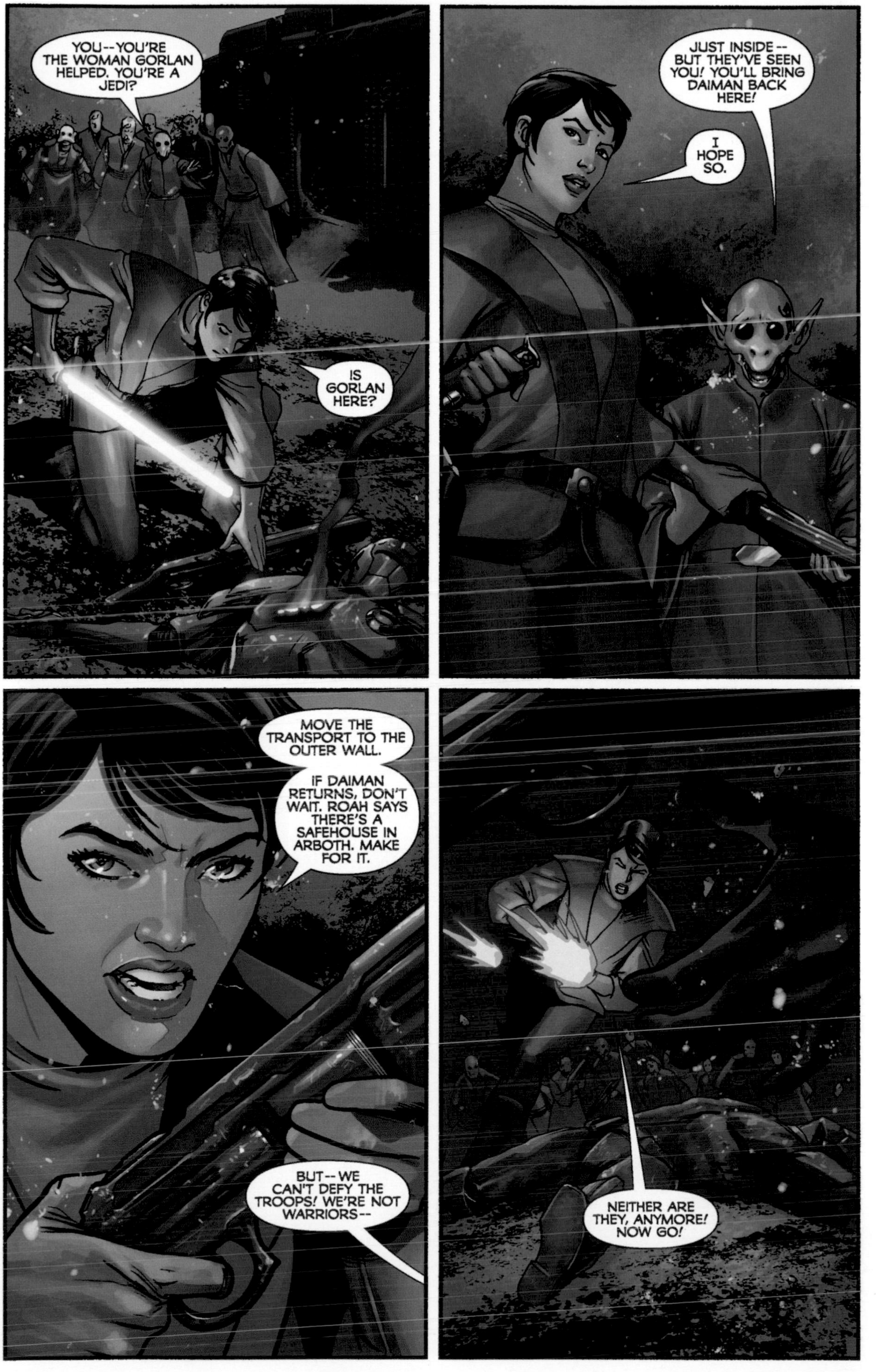
YOU--YOU'RE THE WOMAN GORLAN HELPED. YOU'RE A JEDI?
IS GORLAN HERE?
JUST INSIDE-- BUT THEY'VE SEEN YOU! YOU'LL BRING DAIMAN BACK HERE!
I HOPE SO.
MOVE THE TRANSPORT TO THE OUTER WALL.
IF DAIMAN RETURNS, DON'T WAIT. ROAH SAYS THERE'S A SAFEHOUSE IN ARBOTH. MAKE FOR IT.
BUT--WE CAN'T DEFY THE TROOPS! WE'RE NOT WARRIORS--
NEITHER ARE THEY, ANYMORE! NOW GO!

ROAH? ANEESE?

THEY'RE ALL RIGHT--

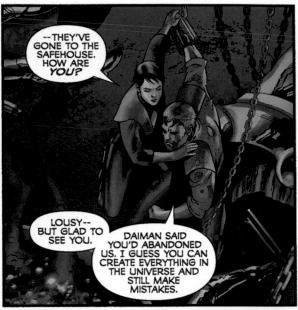

--THEY'VE GONE TO THE SAFEHOUSE. HOW ARE *YOU?*

LOUSY-- BUT GLAD TO SEE YOU.

DAIMAN SAID YOU'D ABANDONED US. I GUESS YOU CAN CREATE EVERYTHING IN THE UNIVERSE AND STILL MAKE MISTAKES.

THAT EXPLAINS HIS BROTHER -- BUT IT'S NOT THE EXPLANATION I WANT.

WHY ARE *YOU* HERE, GORLAN? ARE YOU ODION'S INFORMANT?

YES. *I BROUGHT ODION HERE.*

IT'S NOT WHAT YOU THINK -- BUT, YES. WHAT HAPPENED TO VANNAR AND YOUR FRIENDS WAS *MY FAULT.*

I DIDN'T WANT TO BELIEVE IT -- BUT I KNOW IT NOW.

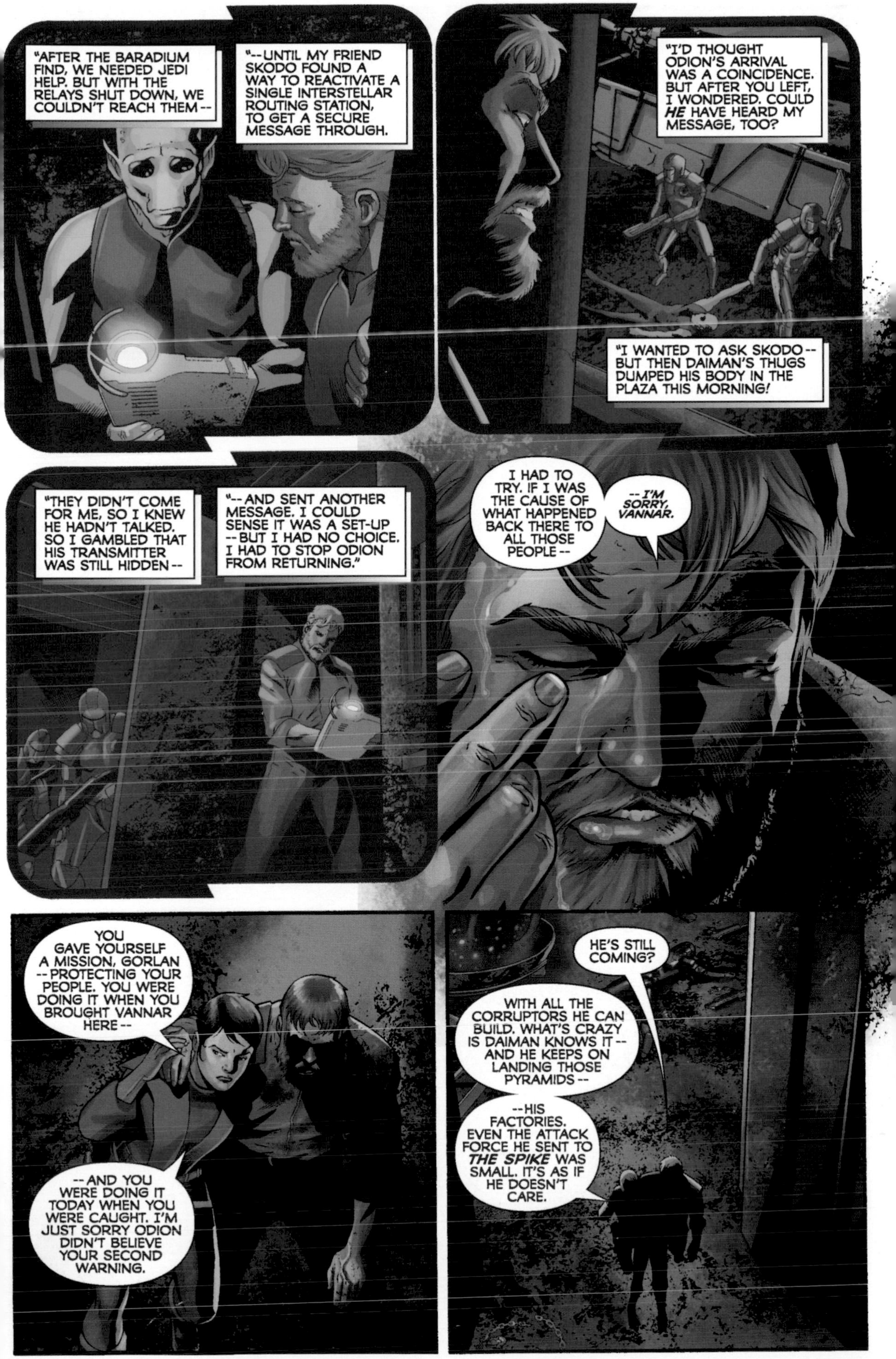
"AFTER THE BARADIUM FIND, WE NEEDED JEDI HELP. BUT WITH THE RELAYS SHUT DOWN, WE COULDN'T REACH THEM --
"-- UNTIL MY FRIEND SKODO FOUND A WAY TO REACTIVATE A SINGLE INTERSTELLAR ROUTING STATION, TO GET A SECURE MESSAGE THROUGH.
"I'D THOUGHT ODION'S ARRIVAL WAS A COINCIDENCE. BUT AFTER YOU LEFT, I WONDERED. COULD HE HAVE HEARD MY MESSAGE, TOO?
"I WANTED TO ASK SKODO -- BUT THEN DAIMAN'S THUGS DUMPED HIS BODY IN THE PLAZA THIS MORNING!
"THEY DIDN'T COME FOR ME, SO I KNEW HE HADN'T TALKED. SO I GAMBLED THAT HIS TRANSMITTER WAS STILL HIDDEN --
"-- AND SENT ANOTHER MESSAGE. I COULD SENSE IT WAS A SET-UP -- BUT I HAD NO CHOICE. I HAD TO STOP ODION FROM RETURNING."
I HAD TO TRY. IF I WAS THE CAUSE OF WHAT HAPPENED BACK THERE TO ALL THOSE PEOPLE --
-- I'M SORRY, VANNAR.
YOU GAVE YOURSELF A MISSION, GORLAN -- PROTECTING YOUR PEOPLE. YOU WERE DOING IT WHEN YOU BROUGHT VANNAR HERE --
-- AND YOU WERE DOING IT TODAY WHEN YOU WERE CAUGHT. I'M JUST SORRY ODION DIDN'T BELIEVE YOUR SECOND WARNING.
HE'S STILL COMING?
WITH ALL THE CORRUPTORS HE CAN BUILD. WHAT'S CRAZY IS DAIMAN KNOWS IT -- AND HE KEEPS ON LANDING THOSE PYRAMIDS --
-- HIS FACTORIES. EVEN THE ATTACK FORCE HE SENT TO THE SPIKE WAS SMALL. IT'S AS IF HE DOESN'T CARE.

GORLAN! DAIMAN'S COMING BACK -- WE JUST HEARD IT ON THE TRANSPORT'S COMM SYSTEM!

THAT'S MY CUE. GET OUT OF HERE. ODION'S ABOUT TO BECOME AN ONLY CHILD.

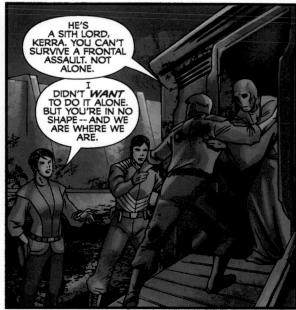

HE'S A SITH LORD, KERRA. YOU CAN'T SURVIVE A FRONTAL ASSAULT. NOT ALONE.

I DIDN'T *WANT* TO DO IT ALONE. BUT YOU'RE IN NO SHAPE -- AND WE ARE WHERE WE ARE.

YOU...YOU *WANT* TO DO IT. DON'T YOU?

YOU DON'T HAVE TO BE A MARTYR, KERRA. I SEE YOU... *THROWING YOURSELF AWAY.*

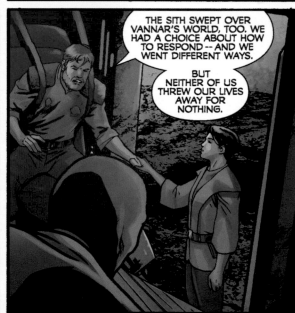

THE SITH SWEPT OVER VANNAR'S WORLD, TOO. WE HAD A CHOICE ABOUT HOW TO RESPOND -- AND WE WENT DIFFERENT WAYS.

BUT NEITHER OF US THREW OUR LIVES AWAY FOR NOTHING.

I HAVE ORDERS. I HAVE A MISSION TO COMPLETE!

BUT KERRA, DON'T YOU REMEMBER? DISABLING THE BARADIUM MINES -- THAT WAS *VANNAR'S* MISSION.

REMEMBER *YOUR* MISSION--

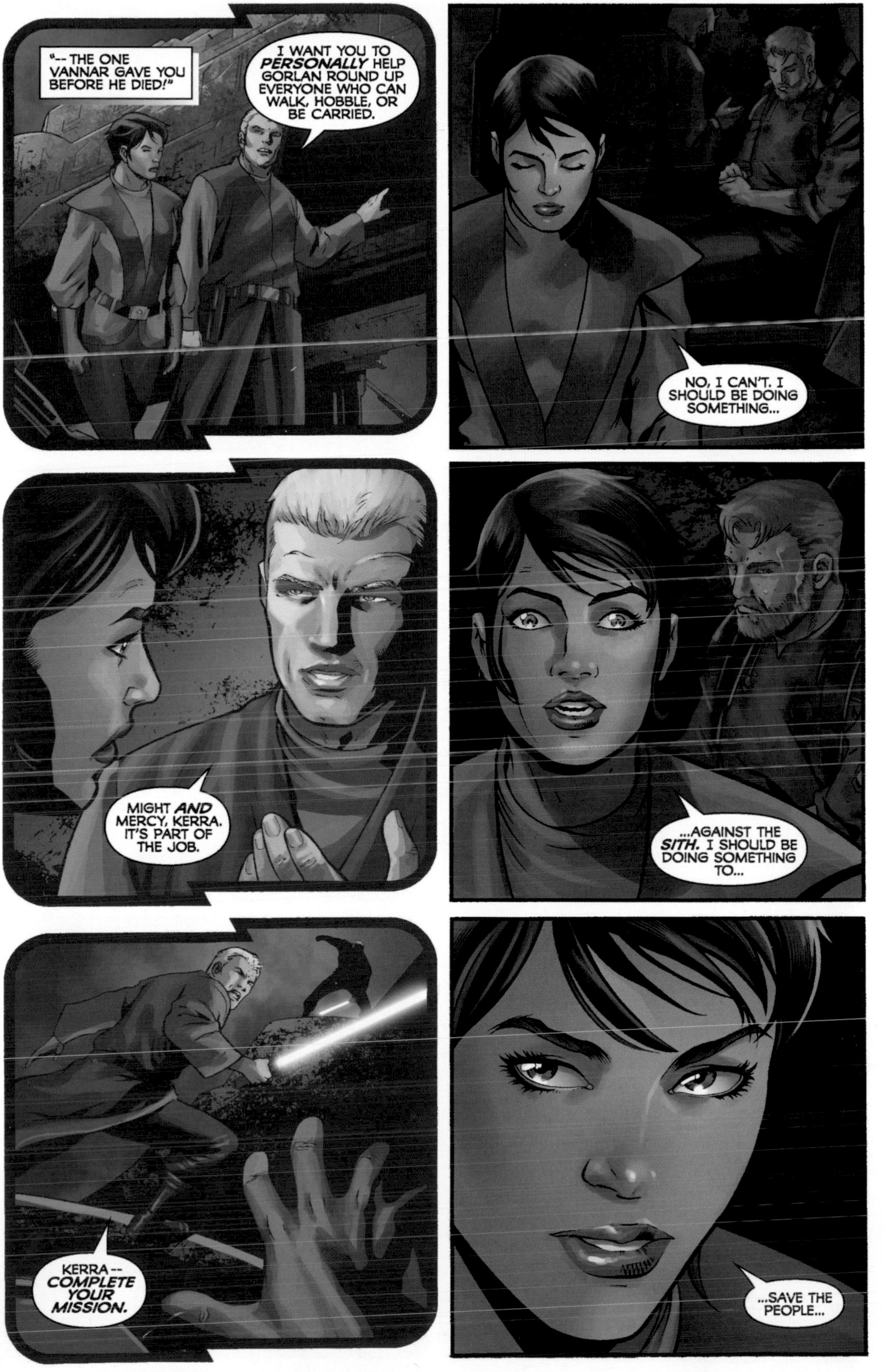
"-- THE ONE VANNAR GAVE YOU BEFORE HE DIED!"
I WANT YOU TO *PERSONALLY* HELP GORLAN ROUND UP EVERYONE WHO CAN WALK, HOBBLE, OR BE CARRIED.
NO, I CAN'T. I SHOULD BE DOING SOMETHING...
MIGHT *AND* MERCY, KERRA. IT'S PART OF THE JOB.
...AGAINST THE *SITH.* I SHOULD BE DOING SOMETHING TO...
KERRA -- *COMPLETE YOUR MISSION.*
...SAVE THE PEOPLE...

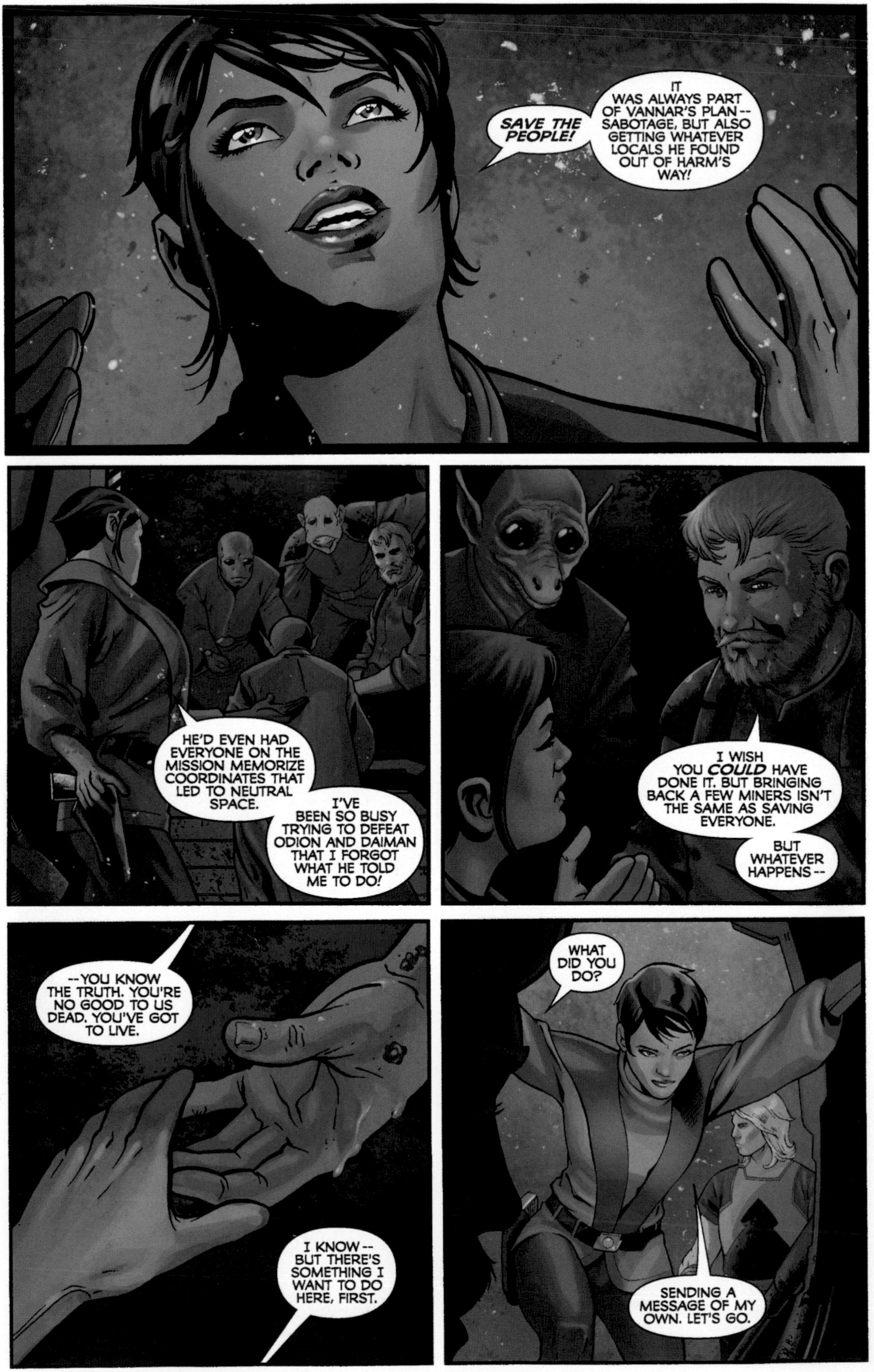

SAVE THE PEOPLE!
IT WAS ALWAYS PART OF VANNAR'S PLAN -- SABOTAGE, BUT ALSO GETTING WHATEVER LOCALS HE FOUND OUT OF HARM'S WAY!
HE'D EVEN HAD EVERYONE ON THE MISSION MEMORIZE COORDINATES THAT LED TO NEUTRAL SPACE.
I'VE BEEN SO BUSY TRYING TO DEFEAT ODION AND DAIMAN THAT I FORGOT WHAT HE TOLD ME TO DO!
I WISH YOU COULD HAVE DONE IT. BUT BRINGING BACK A FEW MINERS ISN'T THE SAME AS SAVING EVERYONE.
BUT WHATEVER HAPPENS --
--YOU KNOW THE TRUTH. YOU'RE NO GOOD TO US DEAD. YOU'VE GOT TO LIVE.
I KNOW -- BUT THERE'S SOMETHING I WANT TO DO HERE, FIRST.
WHAT DID YOU DO?
SENDING A MESSAGE OF MY OWN. LET'S GO.

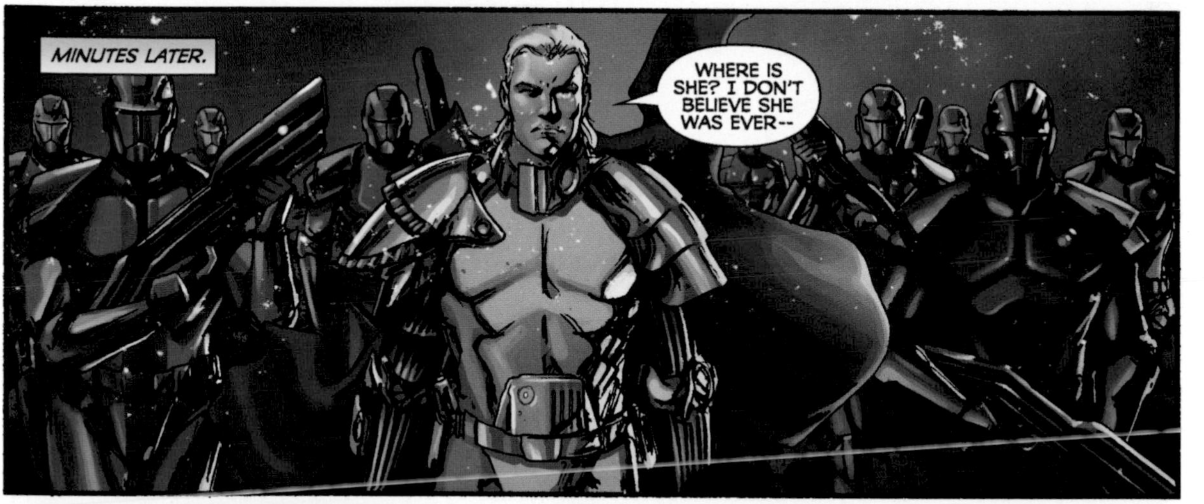
MINUTES LATER.
WHERE IS SHE? I DON'T BELIEVE SHE WAS EVER--

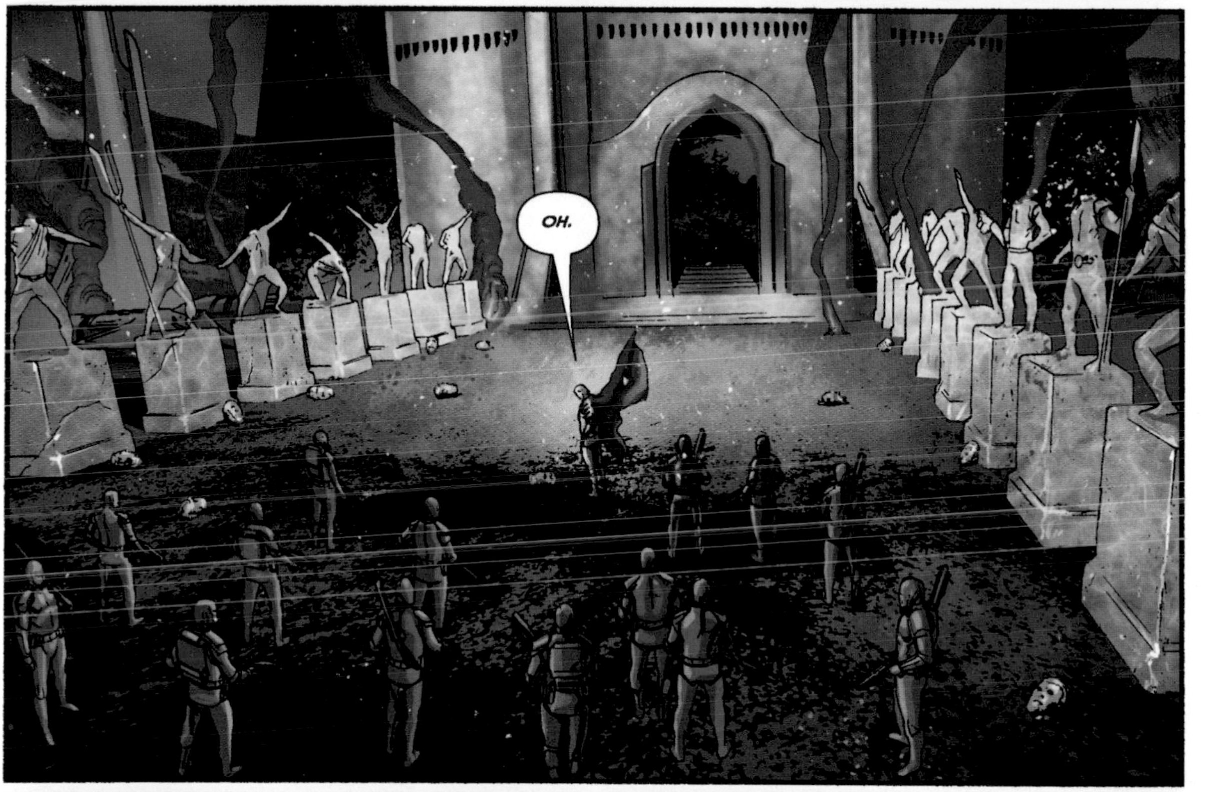
OH.

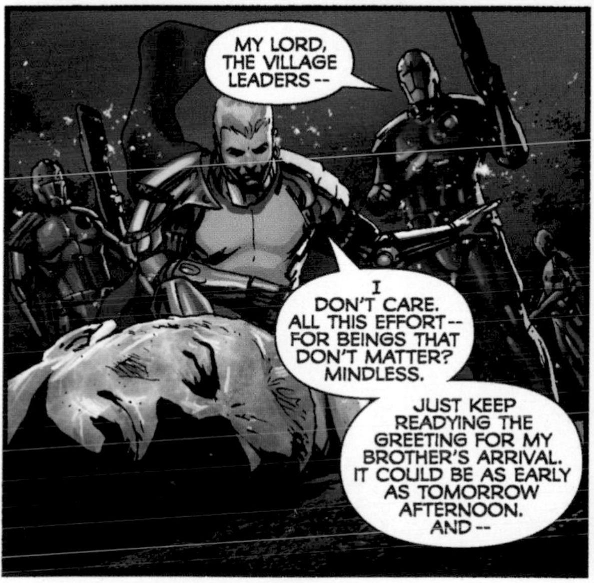
MY LORD, THE VILLAGE LEADERS--
I DON'T CARE. ALL THIS EFFORT-- FOR BEINGS THAT DON'T MATTER? MINDLESS.
JUST KEEP READYING THE GREETING FOR MY BROTHER'S ARRIVAL. IT COULD BE AS EARLY AS TOMORROW AFTERNOON. AND--

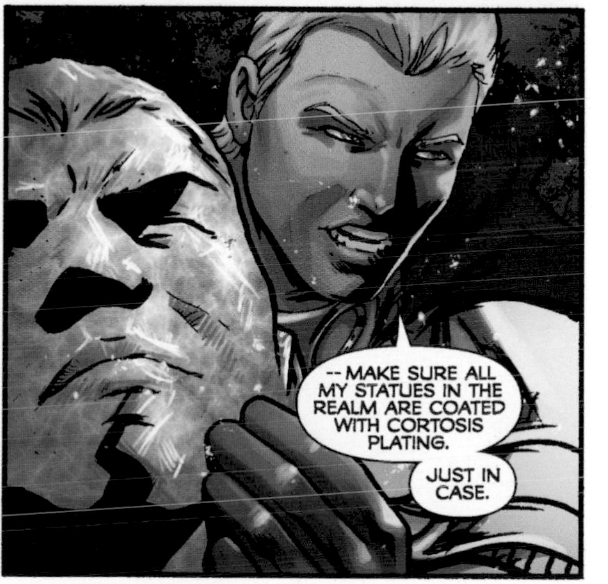
--MAKE SURE ALL MY STATUES IN THE REALM ARE COATED WITH CORTOSIS PLATING.
JUST IN CASE.

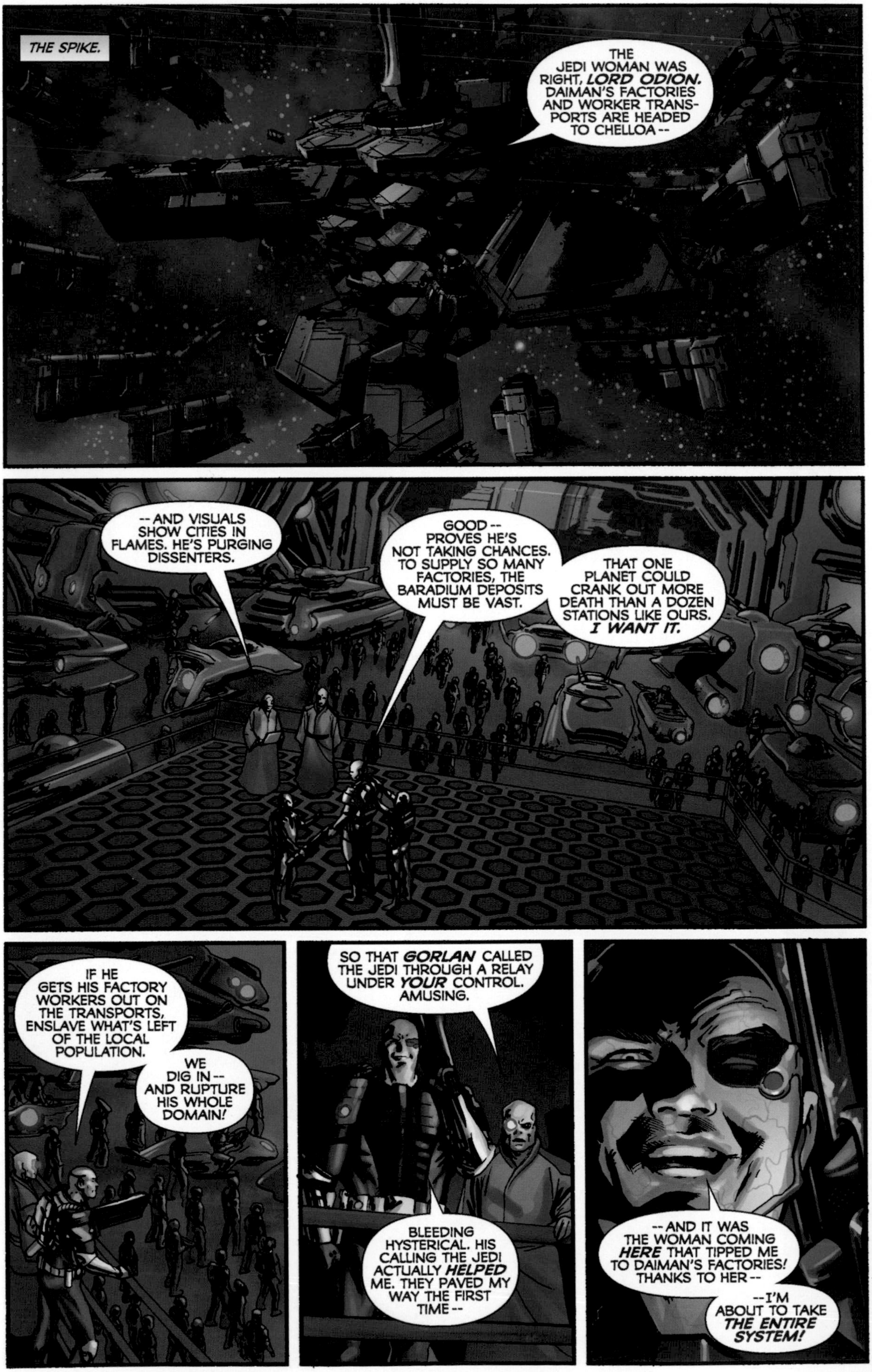

THE SPIKE.
THE JEDI WOMAN WAS RIGHT, LORD ODION. DAIMAN'S FACTORIES AND WORKER TRANSPORTS ARE HEADED TO CHELLOA --
-- AND VISUALS SHOW CITIES IN FLAMES. HE'S PURGING DISSENTERS.
GOOD -- PROVES HE'S NOT TAKING CHANCES. TO SUPPLY SO MANY FACTORIES, THE BARADIUM DEPOSITS MUST BE VAST.
THAT ONE PLANET COULD CRANK OUT MORE DEATH THAN A DOZEN STATIONS LIKE OURS. I WANT IT.
IF HE GETS HIS FACTORY WORKERS OUT ON THE TRANSPORTS, ENSLAVE WHAT'S LEFT OF THE LOCAL POPULATION.
WE DIG IN -- AND RUPTURE HIS WHOLE DOMAIN!
SO THAT GORLAN CALLED THE JEDI THROUGH A RELAY UNDER YOUR CONTROL. AMUSING.
BLEEDING HYSTERICAL. HIS CALLING THE JEDI ACTUALLY HELPED ME. THEY PAVED MY WAY THE FIRST TIME --
-- AND IT WAS THE WOMAN COMING HERE THAT TIPPED ME TO DAIMAN'S FACTORIES! THANKS TO HER --
-- I'M ABOUT TO TAKE THE ENTIRE SYSTEM!

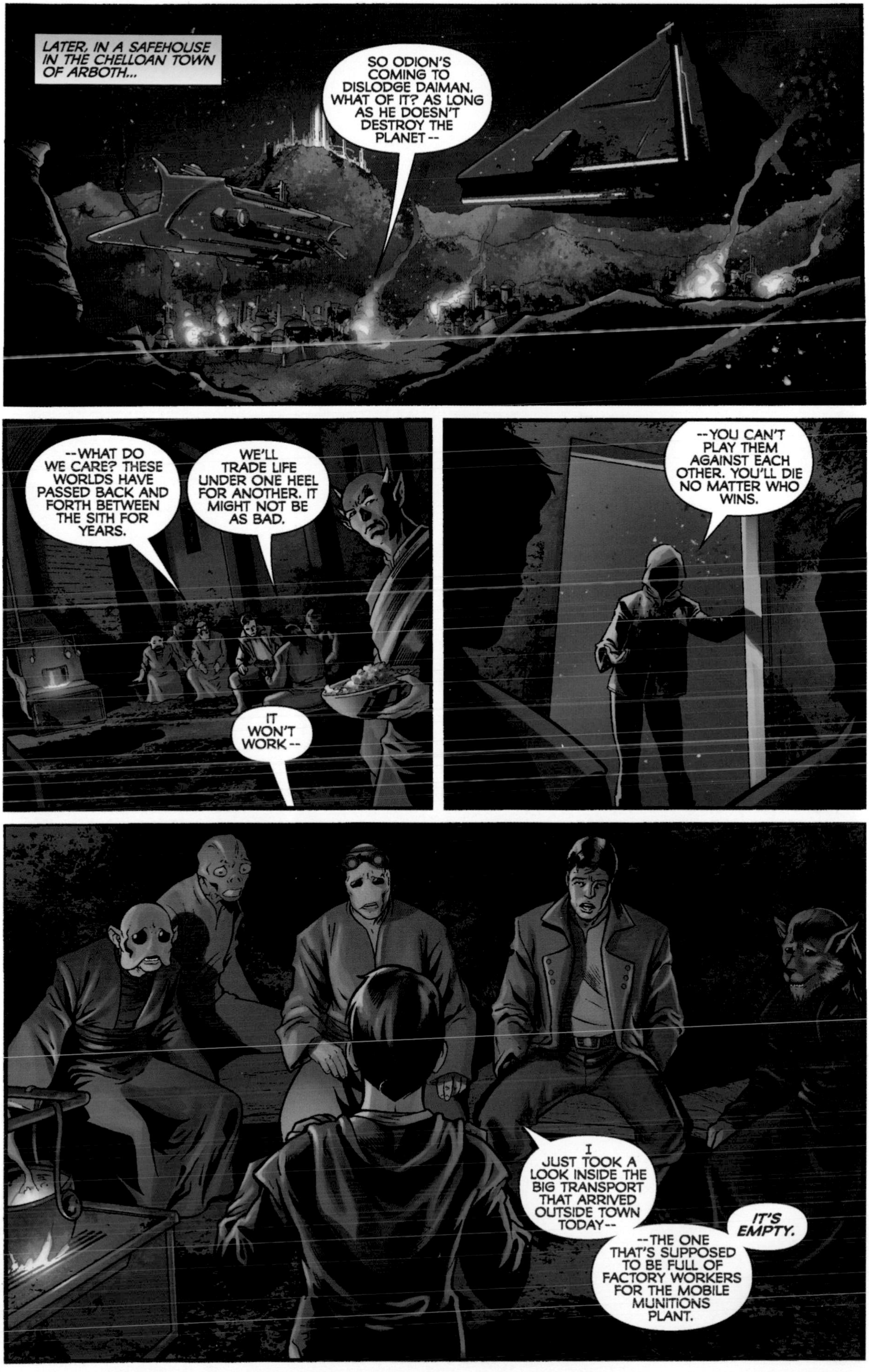
LATER, IN A SAFEHOUSE IN THE CHELLOAN TOWN OF ARBOTH...
SO ODION'S COMING TO DISLODGE DAIMAN. WHAT OF IT? AS LONG AS HE DOESN'T DESTROY THE PLANET --
--WHAT DO WE CARE? THESE WORLDS HAVE PASSED BACK AND FORTH BETWEEN THE SITH FOR YEARS.
WE'LL TRADE LIFE UNDER ONE HEEL FOR ANOTHER. IT MIGHT NOT BE AS BAD.
IT WON'T WORK--
--YOU CAN'T PLAY THEM AGAINST EACH OTHER. YOU'LL DIE NO MATTER WHO WINS.
I JUST TOOK A LOOK INSIDE THE BIG TRANSPORT THAT ARRIVED OUTSIDE TOWN TODAY--
--THE ONE THAT'S SUPPOSED TO BE FULL OF FACTORY WORKERS FOR THE MOBILE MUNITIONS PLANT.
IT'S EMPTY.

MAYBE -- THEY'RE ALREADY INSIDE THE PLANT?

THEY CAN'T BE. THE PYRAMID'S STILL FOLDED UP. THE FACTORY INSIDE ISN'T AIRTIGHT, SO THEY FLY THE WORKERS IN SEPARATELY.

BUT WE SAW WORKERS EXIT THE FIRST TRANSPORT -- THE ONE THAT LANDED OUTSIDE JENITH!

AND THAT'S THE ONLY ONE. NONE OF THE OTHER PARKED TRANSPORTS HAVE ANYONE INSIDE. I CHECKED AS MANY AS I COULD REACH.

THEY'RE ALL EMPTY. I DON'T KNOW WHAT HE HAS PLANNED -- BUT I THINK DAIMAN'S CHANGED HIS MIND.

I SAW DAIMAN THE NIGHT THE FIRST FACTORY ARRIVED. HE *LET* ME ESCAPE TO ODION -- SO ODION WOULD LEARN ABOUT THE FACTORIES.

YOU'RE NOT THE ONLY ONE WHO ACCIDENTALLY DELIVERED A MESSAGE TO ODION, GORLAN.

DAIMAN KNOWS ODION IS COMING TO CONQUER, NOT DESTROY -- AND *THAT'S EXACTLY WHAT DAIMAN WANTS.* I DON'T KNOW WHY --

-- BUT YOU CAN'T CHOOSE ONE SIDE OR THE OTHER. ALL YOU CAN DO IS GET OUT OF THE WAY. HOW MANY SLAVES DID YOU SAY LIVED HERE?

AROUND SIXTY THOUSAND. TEN MINING TOWNS -- PLUS WHATEVER SLAVES LANDED WITH THAT FIRST TRANSPORT.

WHAT, ARE YOU THINKING OF BRINGING A FEW PEOPLE OFFWORLD?

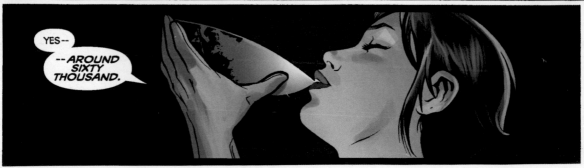

YES --

-- *AROUND SIXTY THOUSAND.*

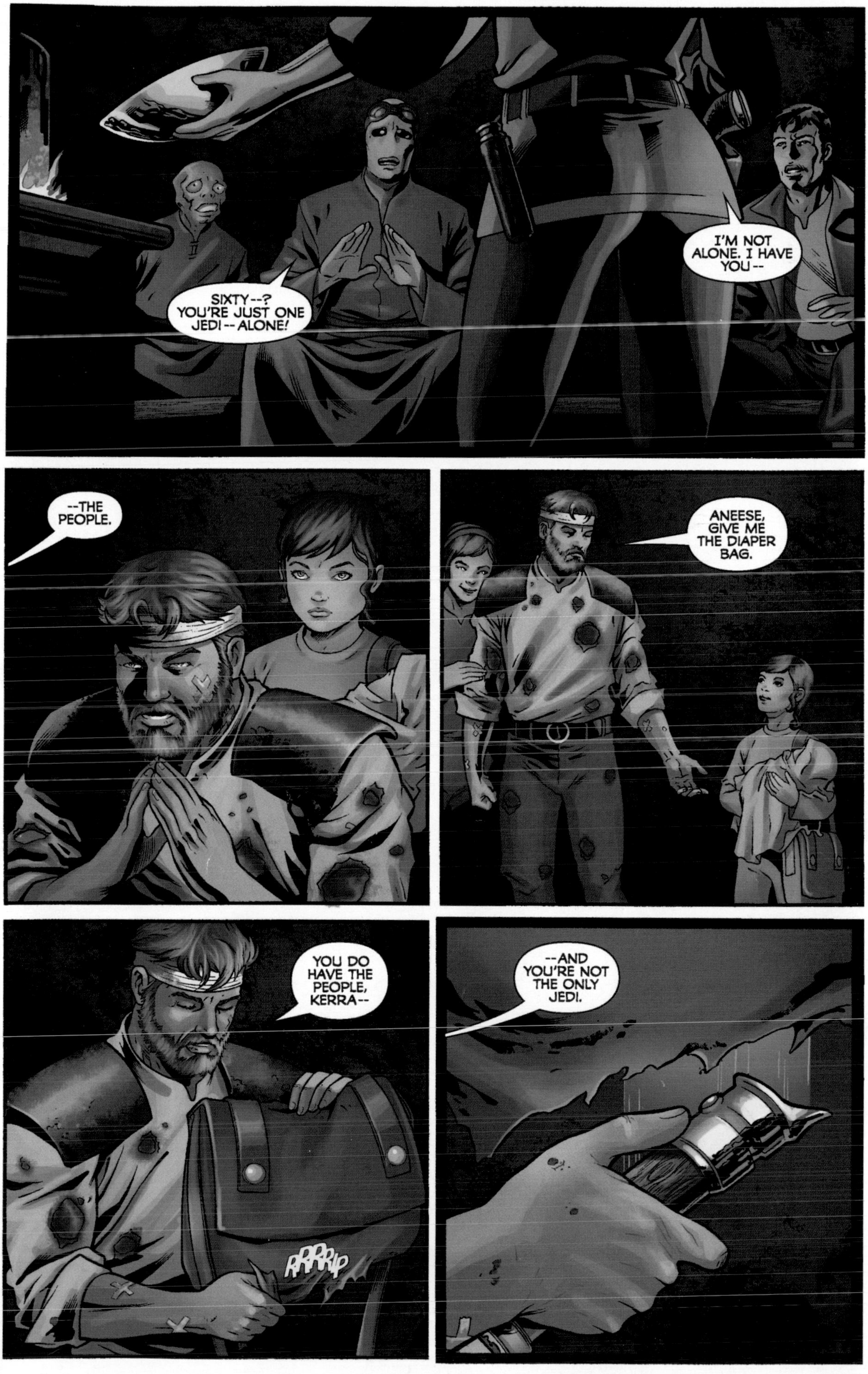
SIXTY--? YOU'RE JUST ONE JEDI--ALONE!
I'M NOT ALONE. I HAVE YOU--
--THE PEOPLE.
ANEESE, GIVE ME THE DIAPER BAG.
YOU DO HAVE THE PEOPLE, KERRA--
RRRRRIP
--AND YOU'RE NOT THE ONLY JEDI.

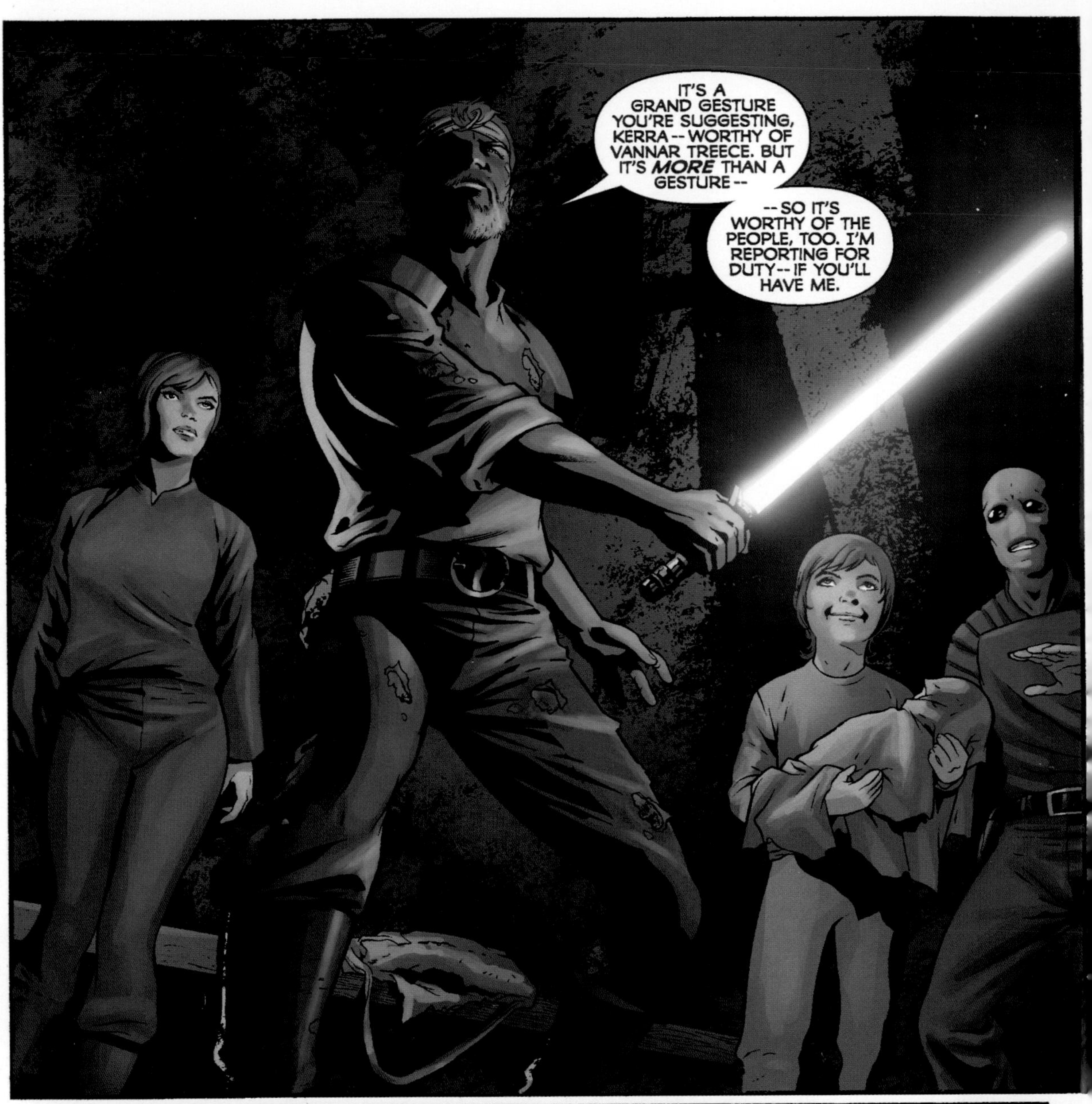
IT'S A GRAND GESTURE YOU'RE SUGGESTING, KERRA -- WORTHY OF VANNAR TREECE. BUT IT'S MORE THAN A GESTURE --
-- SO IT'S WORTHY OF THE PEOPLE, TOO. I'M REPORTING FOR DUTY -- IF YOU'LL HAVE ME.

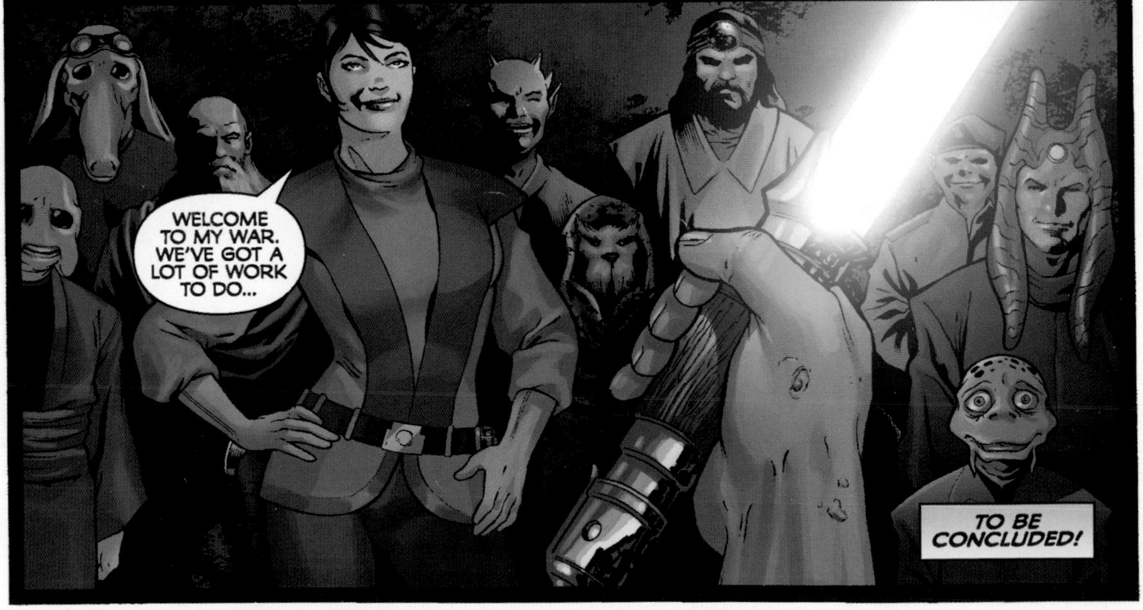
WELCOME TO MY WAR. WE'VE GOT A LOT OF WORK TO DO...
TO BE CONCLUDED!